THE PIT OF THE SERPENT

BY

ROBERT E. HOWARD

British Library Cataloguing-in-Publication Data
A catalogue record for this book is available from the
British Library

Robert E. Howard

Robert Ervin Howard was born in Peaster, Texas in 1906. During his youth, his family moved between a variety of Texan boomtowns, and Howard – a bookish and somewhat introverted child – was steeped in the violent myths and legends of the Old South. Although he loved reading and learning, Howard developed a distinctly Texan, hardboiled outlook on the world. He became a passionate fan of boxing, taking it up at an amateur level, and from the age of nine began to write adventure tales of semi-historical bloodshed. In 1919, when Howard was thirteen, his family moved to the Central Texas hamlet of Cross Plains, where he would stay for the rest of his life.

At fifteen Howard began to read the pulp magazines of the day, and to write more seriously. The December 1922 issue of his high school newspaper featured two of his stories, 'Golden Hope Christmas' and 'West is West'. In 1924 he sold his first piece – a short caveman tale titled 'Spear and Fang' – for $16 to the not-yet-famous *Weird Tales* magazine. He published with the magazine regularly over the next few years. 1929 was a breakout year for Howard, in that the 23-year-old writer began to sell to other magazines, such as *Ghost Stories* and *Argosy*, both of whom had previously sent him hundreds of rejection slips. In 1930, he began a correspondence with weird fiction master H. P. Lovecraft which ran up to his death six years later, and is regarded as one of the great correspondence cycles in all of fantasy literature.

It was partly due to Lovecraft's encouragement that Howard created his most famous character, Conan the Cimmerian. Conan – a barbarian-turned-King during the Hyborian Age, a mythical period of some 12,000 years ago – featured in seventeen *Weird Tales* stories between 1933 and 1936, and is now regarded as having spawned the 'sword and sorcery' genre, making Howard's influence on fantasy literature comparable to that of J. R. R. Tolkien's. The Conan stories have since been adapted many times, most famously in the series of films starring Arnold Schwarzenegger.

Howard was enjoying an all-time high in sales by the beginning of 1936, but he was also deeply upset by the ill health of his mother, who had fallen into a coma. On the morning of June 11, 1936, he asked an attending nurse whether she would ever recover, and the nurse replied negatively. Howard walked to his car, parked outside the family home in Cross Plains, and shot himself. He died eight hours later, aged just thirty.

THE MINUTE I stepped ashore from the Sea Girl, merchantman, I had a hunch that there would be trouble. This hunch was caused by seeing some of the crew of the Dauntless. The men on the Dauntless have disliked the Sea Girl's crew ever since our skipper took their captain to a cleaning on the wharfs of Zanzibar--them being narrow-minded that way. They claimed that the old man had a knuckle-duster on his right, which is ridiculous and a dirty lie. He had it on his left.

Seeing these roughnecks in Manila, I had no illusions about them, but I was not looking for no trouble. I am heavyweight champion of the Sea Girl, and before you make any wisecracks about the non-importance of that title, I want you to come down to the forecastle and look over Mushy Hansen and One-Round Grannigan and Flat-Face O'Toole and Swede Hjonning and the rest of the man-killers that make up the Sea Girl's crew. But for all that, no one can never accuse me of being quarrelsome, and so instead of following my natural instinct and knocking seven or eight of these bezarks for a row, just to be ornery, I avoided them and went to the nearest American bar.

After a while I found myself in a dance hall, and while it is kind of hazy just how I got there, I assure you I had not no great amount of liquor under my belt--some beer, a few whiskeys, a little brandy, and maybe a slug of wine for a chaser like. No, I was the perfect chevalier in all my actions, as was proven when I found myself dancing with the prettiest girl I have yet to see in Manila or elsewhere. She had red lips and black hair, and oh, what a face!

"Say, miss," said I, the soul of politeness, "where have you been all my life?"

"Oooh, la!" said she, with a silvery ripple of laughter. "You Americans say such theengs. Oooh, so huge and strong you are, senyor!"

I let her feel of my biceps, and she give squeals of surprise and pleasure, clapping her little white hands just like a child what has found a new pretty.

"Oooh! You could just snatch little me oop and walk away weeth me, couldn't you, senyor?"

"You needn't not be afraid," said I, kindly. "I am the soul of politeness around frails, and never pull no rough stuff. I have never soaked a woman in my life, not even that dame in Suez that throwed a knife at me. Baby, has anybody ever give you a hint about what knockouts your eyes is?"

"Ah, go 'long," said she, coyly--"Ouch!"

"Did somebody step on your foot?" I ask, looking about for somebody to crown.

"Yes--let's sit theese one out, senyor. Where did you learn to dance?"

"It comes natural, I reckon," I admitted modestly. "I never knew I could till now. This is the first time I ever tried."

From the foregoing you will see that I am carrying on a quiet conversation, not starting nothing with nobody. It is not my fault, what happened.

Me and this girl, whose name is Raquel La Costa, her being Spanish that way, are sitting peacefully at a table and I am just beginning to get started good telling her how her eyes are like dark pools of night (pretty hot, that one; I got it offa Mushy Hansen, who is all poetical like), when I notice her looking over my shoulder at somebody. This irritates me slightly, but I ignore it, and having forgotten what I was saying, my mind being slightly hazy for some reason, I continue:

"Listen, cutey--hey, who are you winkin' at? Oh, somethin' in your eye, you say? All right, as I was sayin', we got a feller named Hansen on board the Sea Girl what writes po'try. Listen to this:

"Oh, the road to glory lay
Over old Manila Bay.
Where the Irish whipped the Spanish
On a sultry summer day."

At this moment some bezark came barging up to our table and, ignoring me, leaned over and leered engagingly at my girl.

"Let's shake a hoof, baby," said this skate, whom I recognized instantly as Bat Slade, champion box fighter of the Dauntless.

Miss La Costa said nothing, and I arose and shoved Slade back from the table.

"The lady is engaged at present, stupid," says I, poking my jaw out. "If you got any business, you better 'tend to it."

"Don't get gay with me, Costigan," says he, nastily. "Since when is dames choosin' gorillas instead of humans?"

By this time quite a crowd had formed, and I restrained my natural indignation and said, "Listen, bird, take that map outa my line uh vision before I bust it."

Bat is a handsome galoot who has a way with the dames, and I knew if he danced one dance with my girl he would figure out some way to do me dirt. I did not see any more of the Dauntless men; on the other hand, I was the only one of the Sea Girl's crew in the joint.

"Suppose we let the lady choose between us," said Bat. Can you beat that for nerve? Him butting in that way and then giving himself equal rights with me. That was too much. With a bellow, I started my left from the hip, but somehow he wasn't there--the shifty crook! I miss by a yard, and he slams me with a left to the nose that knocks me over a chair.

My brain instantly cleared, and I realized that I had been slightly lit. I arose with an irritated roar, but before hostilities could be renewed, Miss La Costa stepped between us.

"Zut," said she, tapping us with her fan. "Zut! What is theese? Am I a common girl to be so insult' by two great tramps who make fight over me in public? Bah! Eef you wanta fight, go out in ze woods or some place where no one make scandal, and wham each other all you want. May ze best man win! I will not be fight over in public, no sir!"

AND WITH THAT she turned back and walked away. At the same time, up came an oily-looking fellow, rubbing his hands together. I mistrust a bird what goes around rubbing his hands together like he was in a state of perpetual self-satisfaction.

"Now, now, boys," said this bezark, "le's do this right! You boys wanta fight. Tut! Tut! Too bad, too bad! But if you gotta fight, le's do it right, that's what I say! Let fellers live together in peace and enmity if they can, but if they gotta fight, let it be did right!"

"Gi' me leeway--and I'll do this blankety-blank right," says I, fairly shaking with rage. It always irritates me to be hit on the nose without a return and in front of ladies.

"Oh, will you?" said Bat, putting up his mitts. "Let's see you get goin', you--"

"Now, now, boys," said the oily bird, "le's do this right! Costigan, will you and Slade fight for me in my club?"

"Anywheres!" I roar. "Bare-knuckles, gloves, or marlin-spikes!"

"Fine," says the oily bird, rubbing his hands worse than ever. "Ah, fine! Ah--um--ah, Costigan, will you fight Slade in the pit of the serpent?"

Now, I should have noticed that he didn't ask Slade if he'd fight, and I saw Slade grin quietly, but I was too crazy with rage to think straight.

"I'll fight him in the pit of Hades with the devil for a referee!" I roared. "Bring on your fight club--ring, deck, or whatever! Let's get goin'."

"That's the way to talk!" says the oily bird. "Come on."

He turned around and started for the exit, and me and Slade and a few more followed him. Had I of thought, I would have seen right off that this was all working too smooth to have happened impromptu, as it were. But I was still seething with rage and in no shape to think properly.

Howthesomever, I did give a few thoughts as to the chances I had against Slade. As for size, I had the advantage. I'm six feet, and Slade is two inches shorter; I am also a few pounds heavier but not enough to make much difference, us being heavyweights that way. But Slade, I knew, was the shiftiest, trickiest leather-slinger in the whole merchant marine. I had never met him for the simple reason that no match-maker in any port would stage a bout between a Sea Girl man and a Dauntless tramp, since that night in Singapore when the bout between Slade and One-Round Grannigan started a free-for-all that plumb wrecked the Wharfside A. C. Slade knocked Grannigan out that night, and Grannigan was then champion slugger aboard the Sea Girl. Later, I beat Grannigan.

As for dope, you couldn't tell much, as usual. I'd won a decision over Boatswain Hagney, the champion of the British Asiatic naval fleet, who'd knocked Slade out in Hong Kong, but on the other hand, Slade had knocked out Mike Leary of the Blue Whale, who'd given me a terrible beating at Bombay.

These cogitations was interrupted at that minute by the oily bird. We had come out of the joint and was standing on the curb. Several autos was parked there, and the crowd piled into them. The oily bird motioned me to get in one, and I done so.

Next, we was speeding through the streets, where the lights was beginning to glow, and I asked no questions, even when we left the business section behind and then went right on through the suburbs and out on a road which didn't appear to be used very much. I said nothing, however.

AT LAST WE stopped at a large building some distance outside the city, which looked more like an ex-palace than anything else. All the crowd alighted, and I done likewise, though I was completely mystified. There was no other houses near, trees grew dense on all sides, the house itself was dark and gloomy-looking. All together I did not like the looks of things but would not let on, with Bat Slade gazing at me in his supercilious way. Anyway, I thought, they are not intending to assassinate me because Slade ain't that crooked, though he would stop at nothing else.

We went up the walk, lined on each side by tropical trees, and into the house. There the oily bird struck a light and we went down in the basement. This was a large, roomy affair, with a concrete floor, and in the center was a pit about seven feet deep, and about ten by eight in dimensions. I did not pay no great attention to it at that time, but I did later, I want to tell you.

"Say," I says, "I'm in no mood for foolishness. What you bring me away out here for? Where's your arena?"

"This here's it," said the oily bird.

"Huh! Where's the ring? Where do we fight?"

"Down in there," says the oily bird, pointing at the pit.

"What!" I yell. "What are you tryin' to hand me?"

"Aw, pipe down," interrupted Bat Slade. "Didn't you agree to fight me in the serpent pit? Stop grouchin' and get your duds off."

"All right," I says, plumb burned up by this deal. "I don't know what you're tryin' to put over, but lemme get that handsome map in front of my right and that's all I want!"

"Grahhh!" snarled Slade, and started toward the other end of the pit. He had a couple of yeggs with him as handlers. Shows his caliber, how he always knows some thug; no matter how crooked the crowd may be, he's never without acquaintances. I looked around and recognized a pickpocket I used to know in Cuba, and asked him to handle me. He said he would, though, he added, they wasn't much a handler could do under the circumstances.

"What kind of a deal have I got into?" I asked him as I stripped. "What kind of a joint is this?"

"This house used to be owned by a crazy Spaniard with more mazuma than brains," said the dip, helping me undress. "He yearned for bull fightin' and the like, and he thought up a brand new one. He rigged up this pit and had his servants go out and bring in all kinds of snakes. He'd put two snakes in the pit and let 'em fight till they killed each other."

"What! I got to fight in a snake den?"

"Aw, don't worry. They ain't been no snakes in there for years. The Spaniard got killed, and the old place went to ruin. They held cock fights here and a few years ago the fellow that's stagin' this bout got the idea of buyin' the house and stagin' grudge fights."

11

"How's he make any money? I didn't see nobody buyin' tickets, and they ain't more'n thirty or forty here."

"Aw, he didn't have no time to work it up. He'll make his money bettin'. He never picks a loser! And he always referees himself. He knows your ship sails tomorrow, and he didn't have no time for ballyhooin'. This fight club is just for a select few who is too sated or too vicious to enjoy a ordinary legitimate prize fight. They ain't but a few in the know--all this is illegal, of course--just a few sports which don't mind payin' for their pleasure. The night Slade fought Sailor Handler they was forty-five men here, each payin' a hundred and twenty-five dollars for admission. Figure it out for yourself."

"Has Slade fought here before?" I ask, beginning to see a light.

"Sure. He's the champion of the pit. Only last month he knocked out Sailor Handler in nine rounds."

Gerusha! And only a few months ago me and the Sailor--who stood six-four and weighed two-twenty--had done everything but knife each other in a twenty-round draw.

"Ho! So that's the way it is," said I. "Slade deliberately come and started trouble with me, knowin' I wouldn't get a square deal here, him bein' the favorite and--"

"No," said the dip, "I don't think so. He just fell for that Spanish frail. Had they been any malice aforethought, word would have circulated among the wealthy sports of the town. As it is, the fellow that owns the joint is throwin' the party free of charge. He didn't have time to work it up. Figure it out--he ain't losing nothin'. Here's two tough sailors wanting to fight a grudge fight--willin' to fight for nothin'. It costs him nothin' to stage the riot. It's a great boost for his club, and he'll win plenty on bets."

The confidence with which the dip said that last gave me cold shivers.

"And who will he bet on?" I asked.

"Slade, of course. Ain't he the pit champion?"

While I was considering this cheering piece of information, Bat Slade yelled at me from the other end of the pit:

"Hey, you blankey dash-dot-blank, ain't you ready yet?"

He was in his socks, shoes and underpants, and no gloves on his hands.

"Where's the gloves?" I asked. "Ain't we goin' to tape our hands?"

"They ain't no gloves," said Slade, with a satisfied grin. "This little riot is goin' to be a bare-knuckle affair. Don't you know the rules of the pit?"

"You see, Costigan," says the oily bird, kinda nervous, "in the fights we put on here, the fighters don't wear no gloves--regular he-man grudge stuff, see?"

"Aw, get goin'!" the crowd began to bellow, having paid nothing to get in and wanting their money's worth. "Lessee some action! What do you think this is? Start somethin'!"

"Shut up!" I ordered, cowing them with one menacing look. "What kind of a deal am I getting here, anyhow?"

"Didn't you agree to fight Slade in the serpent pit?"

"Yes but--"

"Tryin' to back out," said Slade nastily, as usual. "That's like you Sea Girl tramps, you--"

"Blank, exclamation point, and asterisk!" I roared, tearing off my undershirt and bounding into the pit. "Get down in here you blank-blank semicolon, and I'll make you look like the last rose of summer, you--"

Slade hopped down into the pit at the other end, and the crowd began to fight for places at the edge. It was a cinch that some of them was not going to get to see all of it. The sides of the pit were hard and rough, and the floor was the same way, like you'd expect a pit in a concrete floor to be. Of course they was no stools or anything.

"Now then," says the oily bird, "this is a finish fight between Steve Costigan of the Sea Girl, weight one-eighty-eight, and Battling Slade, one-seventy-nine, of the Dauntless, bare-knuckle champion of the Philippine Islands, in as far as he's proved it in this here pit. They will fight three-minute rounds, one minute rest, no limit to the number of rounds.

There will be no decision. They will fight till one of 'em goes out. Referee, me.

"The rules is, nothing barred except hittin' below the belt--in the way of punches, I mean. Break when I say so, and hit on the breakaway if you wanta. Seconds will kindly refrain from hittin' the other man with the water bucket. Ready?"

"A hundred I lay you like a rug", says Slade.

"I see you and raise you a hundred," I snarl.

The crowd began to yell and curse, the timekeeper hit a piece of iron with a six-shooter stock, and the riot was on.

NOW, UNDERSTAND, THIS was a very different fight from any I ever engaged in. It combined the viciousness of a rough-and-tumble with that of a legitimate ring bout. No room for any footwork, concrete to land on if you went down, the uncertain flare of the lights which was hung on the ceiling over us, and the feeling of being crowded for space, to say nothing of thinking about all the snakes which had fought there. Ugh! And me hating snakes that way.

I had figured that I'd have the advantage, being heavier and stronger. Slade couldn't use his shifty footwork to keep out of my way. I'd pin him in a corner and smash him like a cat does a rat. But the bout hadn't been on two seconds before I saw I was all wrong. Slade was just an overgrown Young Griffo. His footwork was second to his ducking and slipping. He had fought in the pit before, and had found that kind of fighting just suited to his peculiar style. He shifted on his feet just enough to keep weaving, while he let my punches go under his arms, around his neck, over his head or across his shoulder.

At the sound of the gong I'd stepped forward, crouching, with both hands going in the only way I knew.

Slade took my left on his shoulder, my right on his elbow, and, blip-blip! his left landed twice to my face. Now I want to tell you that a blow from a bare fist is much different than a blow from a glove, and while less stunning, is more of a punisher in its way. Still, I was used to being hit with bare knuckles, and I kept boring in. I swung a left to the ribs that made Slade grunt, and missed a right in the same direction.

This was the beginning of a cruel, bruising fight with no favor. I felt like a wild animal, when I had time to feel anything but Slade's left, battling down there in the pit, with a ring of yelling, distorted faces leering down at us. The oily bird, referee, leaned over the edge at the risk of falling on top of us, and when we clinched he would yell, "Break, you blank-blanks!" and prod us with a cane. He would dance around the edge of the pit trying to keep in prodding distance, and cussing when the crowd got in his way, which was all the time. There was no room in the pit for him; wasn't scarcely room enough for us.

Following that left I landed, Slade tied me up in a clinch, stamped on my instep, thumbed me in the eye, and swished a right to my chin on the breakaway. Slightly infuriated at this treatment, I curled my lip back and sank a left to the wrist in his midriff. He showed no signs at all of liking this, and retaliated with a left to the body and a right to the side of the head. Then he settled down to work.

He ducked a right and came in close, pounding my waist line with short jolts. When, in desperation, I clinched, he shot a right uppercut between my arms that set me back on my heels. And while I was off balance he threw all his weight against me and scraped me against the wall, which procedure removed a large area of hide from my shoulder. With a roar, I tore loose and threw him the full length of the pit, but, charging after him, he side-stepped somehow and I crashed against the pit wall, head-first. Wham! I was on the floor, with seventeen million stars flashing before me, and the oily bird was counting as fast as he could, "Onetwothreefourfive--"

I bounded up again, not hurt but slightly dizzy. Wham, wham, wham! Bat came slugging in to finish me. I swished loose a right that was labeled T.N.T., but he ducked.

"Look out, Bat! That bird's dangerous!" yelled the oily bird in fright.

"So am I!" snarled Bat, cutting my lip with a straight left and weaving away from my right counter. He whipped a right to the wind that made me grunt, flashed two lefts to my already battered face, and somehow missed with a venomous

17

right. All the time, get me, I was swinging fast and heavy, but it was like hitting at a ghost. Bat had maneuvered me into a corner, where I couldn't get set or defend myself. When I drew back for a punch, my elbow hit the wall. Finally I wrapped both arms around my jaw and plunged forward, breaking through Slade's barrage by sheer weight. As we came together, I threw my arms about him and together we crashed to the floor.

Slade, being the quicker that way, was the first up, and hit me with a roundhouse left to the side of the head while I was still on one knee.

"Foul!" yells some of the crowd.

"Shut up!" bellowed the oily bird. "I'm refereein' this bout!"

As I found my feet, Slade was right on me and we traded rights. Just then the gong sounded. I went back to my end of the pit and sat down on the floor, leaning my back against the wall. The dip peered over the edge.

"Anything I can do?" said he.

"Yeah," said I, "knock the daylights out of the blank-blank that's pretendin' to referee this bout."

Meanwhile the aforesaid blank-blank shoved his snoot over the other end of the pit, and shouted anxiously, "Slade, you reckon you can take him in a couple more rounds?"

"Sure," said Bat. "Double your bets; triple 'em. I'll lay him in the next round."

"You'd better!" admonished this fair-minded referee.

"How can he get anybody to bet with him?" I asked.

"Oh," says the dip, handing me down a sponge to wipe off the blood, "some fellers will bet on anything. For instance, I just laid ten smackers on you, myself."

"That I'll win?"

"Naw; that you'll last five rounds."

AT THIS MOMENT the gong sounded and I rushed for the other end of the pit, with the worthy intention of effacing Slade from the face of the earth. But, as usual, I underestimated the force of my rush and the length of the pit. There didn't seem to be room enough for Slade to get out of my way, but he solved this problem by dropping on his knees, and allowing me to fall over him, which I did.

"Foul!" yelled the dip. "He went down without bein' hit!"

"Foul my eye!" squawked the oily bird. "A blind man could tell he slipped, accidental."

We arose at the same time, me none the better for my fiasco. Slade took my left over his shoulder and hooked a left to the body. He followed this with a straight right to the mouth and a left hook to the side of the head. I clinched and clubbed him with my right to the ribs until the referee prodded us apart.

Again Slade managed to get me into a corner. You see, he was used to the dimensions whereas I, accustomed to a

19

regular ring, kept forgetting about the size of the blasted pit. It seemed like with every movement I bumped my hip or shoulder or scraped my arms against the rough cement of the walls. To date, Slade hadn't a mark to show he'd been in a fight, except for the bruise on his ribs. What with his thumbing and his straight lefts, both my eyes were in a fair way to close, my lips were cut, and I was bunged up generally, but was not otherwise badly hurt.

I fought my way out of the corner, and the gong found us slugging toe to toe in the center of the pit, where I had the pleasure of staggering Bat with a left to the temple. Not an awful lot of action in that round; mostly clinching.

The third started like a whirlwind. At the tap of the gong Slade bounded from his end and was in mine before I could get up. He slammed me with a left and right that shook me clean to my toes, and ducked my left. He also ducked a couple of rights, and then rammed a left to my wind which bent me double. No doubt--this baby could hit!

I came up with a left swing to the head, and in a wild mix-up took four right and left hooks to land my right to the ribs. Slade grunted and tried to back-heel me, failing which he lowered his head and butted me in the belly, kicked me on the shin, and would have did more, likely, only I halted the proceedings temporarily by swinging an overhand right to the back of his neck which took the steam out of him for a minute.

We clinched, and I never saw a critter short of a octopus which could appear to have so many arms when clinching. He always managed to not only tie me up and render me helpless for the time being, but to stamp on my insteps, thumb me in the eye and pound the back of my neck with the edge of his hand. Add to this the fact that he frequently shoved me against the wall, and you can get a idea what kind of a bezark I was fighting. My superior weight and bulk did not have no advantage. What was needed was skill and speed, and the fact that Bat was somewhat smaller than me was an advantage to him.

Still, I was managing to hand out some I punishment. Near the end of that round Bat had a beautiful black eye and some more bruises on his ribs. Then it happened. I had plunged after him, swinging; he sidestepped out of the corner, and the next instant was left-jabbing me to death while I floundered along the wall trying to get set for a smash.

I swished a right to his body, and while I didn't think it landed solid, he staggered and dropped his hands slightly. I straightened out of my defensive crouch and cocked my right, and, simultaneous, I realized I had been took. Slade had tricked me. The minute I raised by chin in this careless manner, he beat me to the punch with a right that smashed my head back against the wall, laying open the scalp. Dazed and only partly conscious of what was going on I rebounded right into Slade, ramming my jaw flush into his left. Zam! At the same instant I hooked a trip-hammer right under his heart, and we hit the floor together.

Zowie! I could hear the yelling and cursing as if from a great distance, and the lights on the ceiling high above seemed dancing in a thick fog. All I knew was that I had to get back on my feet as quick as I could.

"One--two--three--four," the oily bird was counting over the both of us, "five--Bat, you blank-blank, get up!--Six--seven--Bat, blast it, get your feet under you!--eight--Juan, hit that gong! What kind of a timekeeper are you?"

"The round ain't over yet!" yelled the dip, seeing I had begun to get my legs under me.

"Who's refereein' this?" roared the oily bird, jerking out a .45. "Juan, hit that gong!--Nine!"

Juan hit the gong and Bat's seconds hopped down into the pit and dragged him to his end, where they started working over him. I crawled back to mine. Splash! The dip emptied a bucket of water over me. That freshened me up a lot.

"How you comin'?" he asked.

"Great!" said I, still dizzy. "I'll lay this bird like a rug in the next round! For honor and the love of a dame! 'Oh, the road to glory lay--'"

"I've seen 'em knocked even more cuckoo," said the dip, tearing off a cud of tobacco.

THE FOURTH! SLADE came up weakened, but with fire in his eye. I was all right, but my legs wouldn't work like they should. Slade was in far better condition. Seeing this, or probably feeling that he was weakening, he threw caution to the winds and rushed in to slug with me.

The crowd went crazy. Left-right-left-right! I was taking four to one, but mine carried the most steam. It couldn't last long at this rate.

The oily bird was yelling advice and dashing about the pit's edge like a lunatic. We went into a clinch, and he leaned over to prod us apart as usual. He leaned far over, and I don't know if he slipped or somebody shoved him. Anyway, he crashed down on top of us just as we broke and started slugging. He fell between us, stopped somebody's right with his chin, and flopped, face down--through for the night!

By mutual consent, Bat and me suspended hostilities, grabbed the fallen referee by his neck and the slack of his pants, and hove him up into the crowd. Then, without a word, we began again. The end was in sight.

Bat suddenly broke and backed away. I followed, swinging with both hands. Now I saw the wall was at his back. Ha! He couldn't duck now! I shot my right straight for his face. He dropped to his knees. Wham! My fist just cleared the top of his skull and crashed against the concrete wall.

I heard the bones shatter and a dark tide of agony surged up my arm, which dropped helpless at my side. Slade was up and springing for me, but the torture I was in made me forget all about him. I was nauseated, done up--out on my feet, if you get what I mean. He swung his left with everything he had--my foot slipped in some blood on the floor--his left landed high on the side of my skull instead of my jaw. I went down, but I heard him squawk and looked up to see him dancing and wringing his left hand.

The knockdown had cleared my brain somewhat. My hand was numb and not hurting so much, and I realized that Bat had broke his left hand on my skull like many a man has did. Fair enough! I came surging up, and Bat, with the light of desperation in his eyes, rushed in wide open, staking everything on one right swing.

I stepped inside it, sank my left to the wrist in his midriff, and brought the same hand up to his jaw. He staggered, his arms fell, and I swung my left flush to the button with everything I had behind it. Bat hit the floor.

About eight men shoved their snoots over the edge and started counting, the oily bird being still out. They wasn't all counting together, so somehow I managed to prop myself up against the wall, not wanting to make no mistake, until the last man had said "ten!" Then everything began to whirl, and I flopped down on top of Slade and went out like a candle.

LET'S PASS OVER the immediate events. I don't remember much about them anyhow. I slept until the middle of the next afternoon, and I know the only thing that dragged me out of the bed where the dip had dumped me was the knowledge that the Sea Girl sailed that night and that Raquel La Costa probably would be waiting for the victor--me.

Outside the joint where I first met her, who should I come upon but Bat Slade!

"Huh!" says I, giving him the once over. "Are you able to be out?"

"You ain't no beauty yourself," he retorted.

I admit it. My right was in a sling, both eyes was black, and I was generally cut and bruised. Still, Slade had no right to give himself airs. His left was all bandaged, he too had a black eye, and moreover his features was about as battered as mine. I hope it hurt him as much to move as it did me. But he had the edge on me in one way--he hadn't rubbed as much hide off against the walls.

"Where's that two hundred we bet?" I snarled.

"Heh, heh!" sneered he. "Try and get it! They told me I wasn't counted out officially. The referee didn't count me out. You didn't whip me."

"Let the money go, you dirty, yellow crook," I snarled, "but I whipped you, and I can prove it by thirty men. What you doin' here, anyway?"

"I come to see my girl."

"Your girl? What was we fightin' about last night?"

"Just because you had the sap's luck to knock me stiff don't mean Raquel chooses you," he answered savagely. "This time, she names the man she likes, see? And when she does, I want you to get out!"

"All right," I snarled. "I whipped you fair and can prove it. Come in here; she'll get a chance to choose between us, and if she don't pick the best man, why, I can whip you all over again. Come on, you--"

Saying no more, we kicked the door open and went on in. We swept the interior with a eagle glance, and then sighted Raquel sitting at a table, leaning on her elbows and gazing soulfully into the eyes of a handsome bird in the uniform of a Spanish naval officer.

We barged across the room and come to a halt at her table. She glanced up in some surprise, but she could not have been blamed had she failed to recognize us.

"Raquel," said I, "we went forth and fought for your fair hand just like you said. As might be expected, I won. Still, this incomprehensible bezark thinks that you might still have some lurkin' fondness for him, and he requires to hear from your own rosy lips that you love another--meanin' me, of course. Say the word and I toss him out. My ship sails tonight, and I got a lot to say to you."

"Santa Maria!" said Raquel. "What ees theese? What kind of a bizness is theese, you two tramps coming looking like theese and talking gibberish? Am I to blame eef two great tramps go pound each other's maps, ha? What ees that to me?"

"But you said--" I began, completely at sea, "you said, go fight and the best man--"

"I say, may the best man win! Bah! Did I geeve any promise? What do I care about Yankee tramps what make the fist-fight? Bah! Go home and beefsteak the eye. You insult me, talking to me in public with the punch' nose and bung' up face."

"Then you don't love either of us?" said Bat.

"Me love two gorillas? Bah! Here is my man--Don Jose y Balsa Santa Maria Gonzales."

She then gave a screech, for at that moment Bat and me hit Don Jose y Balsa Santa Maria Gonzales simultaneous, him with the right and me with the left. And then, turning our backs on the dumfounded Raquel, we linked arms and, stepping over the fallen lover, strode haughtily to the door and vanished from her life.

"AND THAT," SAID I, as we leaned upon the bar to which we had made our mutual and unspoke agreement, "ends our romance, and the glory road leads only to disappointment and hokum."

"Women," said Bat gloomily, "are the bunk."

"Listen," said I, remembering something, "how about that two hundred you owe me?"

"What for?"

"For knockin' you cold."

"Steve," said Bat, laying his hand on my shoulder in brotherly fashion, "you know I been intendin' to pay you that all along. After all, Steve, we are seamen together, and we have just been did dirt by a woman of another race. We are both American sailors, even if you are a harp, and we got to stand by each other. Let bygones be bygones, says I. The fortunes of war, you know. We fought a fair, clean fight, and you was lucky enough to win. Let's have one more drink and then part in peace an' amity."

"You ain't holdin' no grudge account of me layin' you out?" I asked, suspiciously.

"Steve," said Bat, waxing oratorical, "all men is brothers, and the fact that you was lucky enough to crown me don't alter my admiration and affection. Tomorrow we will be sailin' the high seas, many miles apart. Let our thoughts of each other be gentle and fraternal. Let us forgit old feuds and old differences. Let this be the dawn of a new age of brotherly affection and square dealin'."

"And how about my two hundred?"

"Steve, you know I am always broke at the end of my shore leave. I give you my word I'll pay you them two hundred smackers. Ain't the word of a comrade enough?

Now le's drink to our future friendship and the amicable relations of the crews of our respective ships. Steve, here's my hand! Let this here shake be a symbol of our friendship. May no women ever come between us again! Good-bye, Steve! Good luck! Good luck!"

And so saying, we shook and turned away. That is, I turned and then whirled back as quick as I could--just in time to duck the right swing he'd started the minute my back was turned, and to knock him cold with a bottle I snatched off the bar.

THE END